TESTING MISS MALARKEY

CAMPBELL —

O'Malley

"ISaac; ELA SOPHIA SETH"

Marks

Plutt

Connor~dude

Baltimore Maryland

Big Noah

To grandson Joshua Sidney Finchler, may your life be filled with as much joy as you have brought to ours. —J. F.

To Big Pat and the Vizzard Family. —K. O.

ISBN 0-439-20100-4

Text copyright © 2000 by Judy Finchler.
Illustrations copyright © 2000 by Kevin O'Malley.
All rights reserved.
Published by Scholastic Inc., 555 Broadway, New York, NY 10012,
by arrangement with Walker Publishing Company, Inc.
SCHOLASTIC and associated logos are trademarks and/or registered
trademarks of Scholastic Inc.

12 11 10 9 8 7 6 5 4 3 2   1 2 3 4 5 6/0

Printed in the U.S.A.   14

First Scholastic printing, January 2001

All the characters and events portrayed in this work are fictitious.

Book design by Sophie Ye Chin

TESTING MISS MALARKEY

Judy Finchler
Illustrations by Kevin O'Malley

SCHOLASTIC INC.
New York Toronto London Auckland Sydney
Mexico City New Delhi Hong Kong

Miss Malarkey is a good teacher. Usually she's really nice. But a couple of weeks ago she started acting a little weird. She started talking about THE TEST: The Instructional Performance Through Understanding test. I think Miss Malarkey said it was called the "I.P.T.U." test.

But Miss Malarkey said THE TEST wasn't that important. She said it wouldn't affect our report cards. It wouldn't mean extra homework. And if we didn't do well, we'd still go on to the next grade.

At recess we played Multiplication Mambo. Each class got new CD roms called "There's Something About Decimals." After lunch we played Funny Phonics. Miss Malarkey said you never know what's going to be on THE TEST.

The closer we got to "THE TEST DAY," the weirder things got. When I brought the attendance sheets to the office, I heard Principal Wiggins yelling about pencils.

The cafeteria lady, Mrs. Slopdown, took away the potato chips and served only fish.

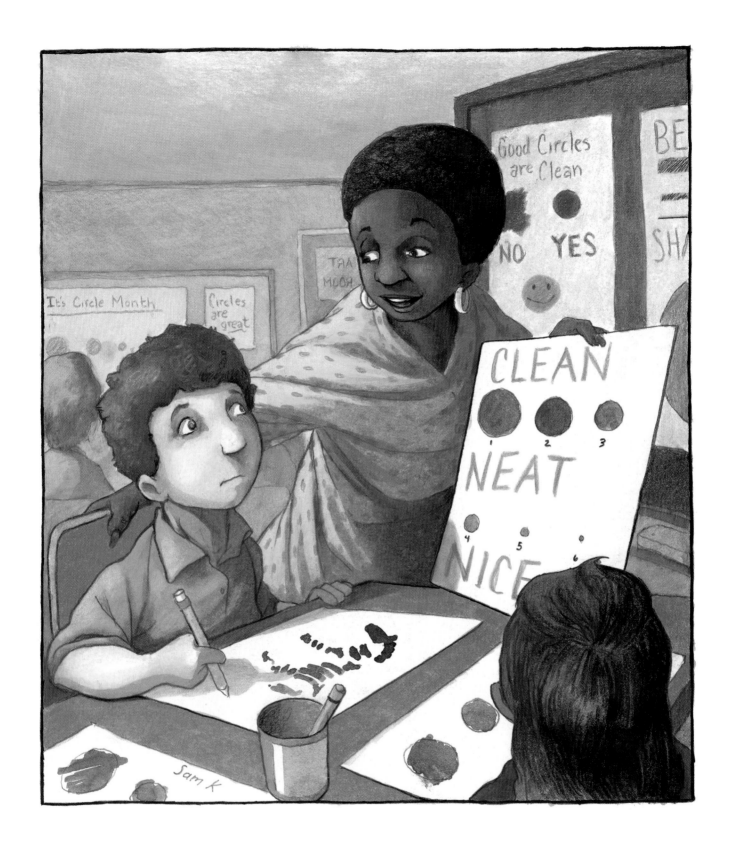

In art we each made posters about THE TEST. Mrs. Magenta also showed us how to color in all those little circles they put on tests.

During gym we didn't play baseball or even exercise. Mr. Fittanuff said we had to prepare our minds and bodies for THE TEST. We all learned something about meditating and about something called "yogurt." Like I said, things were getting pretty weird at school. I got to thinking THE TEST was sort of important.

Even my mom knew about THE TEST. When she read me my bedtime story, I had to complete a ditto and give the main idea before I could go to sleep.

Mom started making me eat a really big breakfast. For lunch she packed me a Power Bar 2000. When I got to school, I traded Adam for a fat-free bran muffin. He traded with Hanna for a Baggie of carrot sticks. Hanna didn't want the Power Bar so she asked her best friend, Meredith, if she would trade for her apple. Somehow someone must have wanted the apple, and I'm not sure what happened but I had the Power Bar 2000 again.

One night Mom took me to a PTA meeting. A man was there talking about THE TEST. He wasn't a teacher or a parent or even the principal, but whoever he was he seemed to think THE TEST was very important. So did the parents.

The day of THE TEST the janitor, Mr. Surley, closed off the whole hallway. You couldn't even walk down it unless you had a pass. And you had to whisper. Miss Malarkey had to whisper the secret password to Mr. Surley before she could go to Room 10.

TESTERS ONLY

NO TALKING!!

IPTU -TESTING- -AREA-

BE PREPARED

DANGER

That morning there were more teachers than kids waiting for the nurse.

Miss Malarkey's job was to hand out the No. 2 pencils and the scratch paper. She looked like she didn't get enough sleep. Principal Wiggins was keeping the time. We couldn't even touch THE TEST until he waved the flag. When it was time to start, he waved the flag so hard, something happened to his hair.

① Stay
② Breathe
③ Read
carefull
④ Be ne
⑤ Clean c

THE TEST took forever.
It took two whole
days. My friend Carmine
got in trouble for not
using his scratch paper
the right way. I thought
his ninja warrior looked
pretty good, though.

Miss Malarkey caught Barry with his
baseball cards.

Morgan got a stomachache and had to go to the nurse. The hall monitor gave her such a hard time, she threw up right in the hall.

When Miss Malarkey said to erase all your pencil marks, Janet erased her whole test.

Principal Wiggins was in the room for a while, but he had a stomachache and had to go to the nurse. I hope he didn't throw up in the hall too.

After THE TEST everybody got prizes and had treats and we got extra recess. Even Steven, who fell asleep two times during THE TEST. Miss Malarkey looked wiped out, and she didn't even take THE TEST.

It's been a long time since we took THE TEST. Things are back to normal. Principal Wiggins isn't yelling quite as much. The cafeteria lady started serving potato chips again. Mom's packing me good old peanut butter and jelly sandwiches. And Miss Malarkey is letting her fingernails grow real long. I guess THE TEST really wasn't that important after all.